SMILES
OF THE WORLD
Celebrating Traditions

HOLA

KON'NI

MARHABA

CIAO

Olá

Hailō

HEI

HEJ

HELLO

Nǐ hǎo

Bonghjornu

SMILES OF THE WORLD
Celebrating Traditions

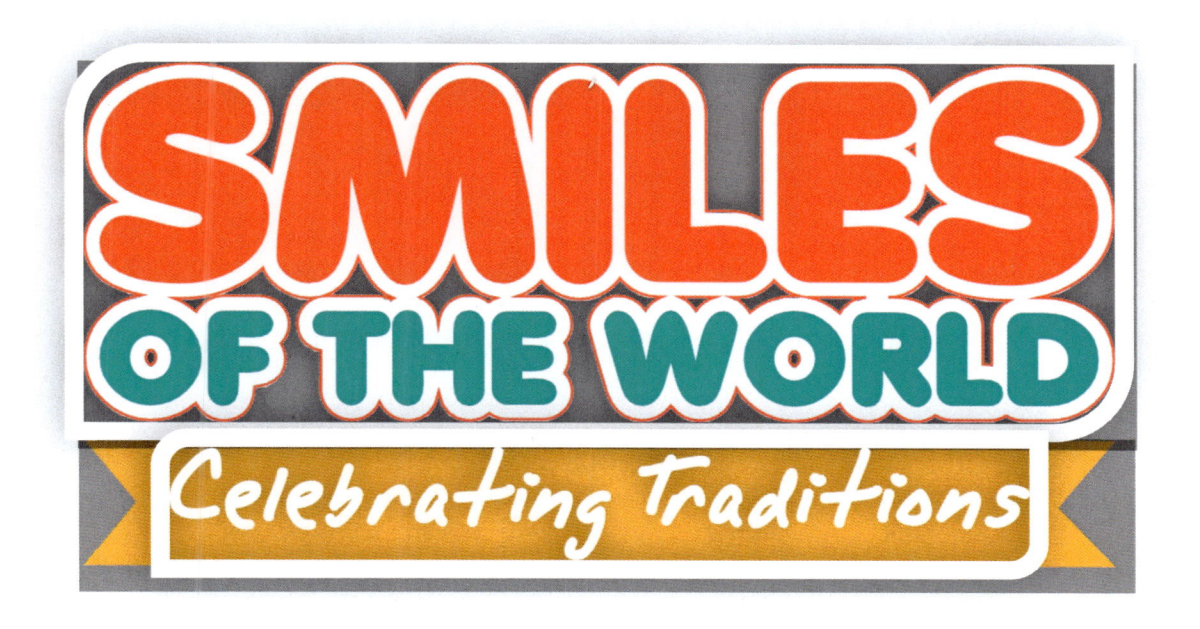

By Dina Al-Sabawi • Illustrated by Yujie Studios

Copyright © 2020 Dina Al-Sabawi
Illustrations Copyright © Yujie Studios

All rights reserved. No part of this publication may be reproduced, distributed or transmitted in any form or by any means, including photocopying, recording, or other electronic or mechanical methods, without written permission from the publisher, except in the case of quotations embodied in non-commercial uses.

Printed in the USA ∘ISBN 9798698677253
Design by Dina Al-Sabawi ∘ Text set in Daytona Pro Light

This book belongs to:

_____

"For my parents, Mohamed, Kyce & Kenan."
Love, Dina

We all have smiles that shine

bright like a light.

We all have eyes that twinkle

and sprinkle.

We all have noses that smell flowers after the April showers.

we all have hands that play

and sway.

We all have feet that tromp

and stomp.

We can use our smiles to spread cheer.

We can use our eyes to see

with love instead of fear.

we can use our noses to smell spices of different scents.

We can use our hands to share and give presents.

We can use our feet to walk side by side.

We all look beautiful and different,

but share the same wonderful inside.

GOOD BYE

Hyvästi

FARVEL

BLESS

TOFA

Tạm biệt

Adiós

SELAMAT TINGGAL

VALE

Zàijiàn

Manufactured by Amazon.ca
Bolton, ON